To Marcus,
many Blessings for a
Life Full of Miracles!
Love,

This book
is dedicated to
Unity

We Are One

Written and illustrated
by
Jennifer Black

www.worldofweareone.com

We are all one but different.

Different but the same.

flower girl cat

Created by the one light,

we are each given a name.

Some of us are insects,

some are animals too,

some of us are people,

just like me and you.

We all share the same moon,

we also share one sun,

we all live on planet earth,

the air we breathe is one.

Some of us live where it is cold,

some of us live where it is hot,

some of us live in the deep blue sea,

some of us live in one spot.

So one thing to remember is...
We are all one but different.
Different but the same.

butterfly

spider

lion

Created by the one light,
we are each given a name.

Some of us are fluffy,

some of us are tall,

some of us have feathers,

some of us are small.

We all have different feelings,

we all make different sounds,

we all see things individually,

like what makes the world go around.

The light that shines within our hearts
is the love that makes us care.

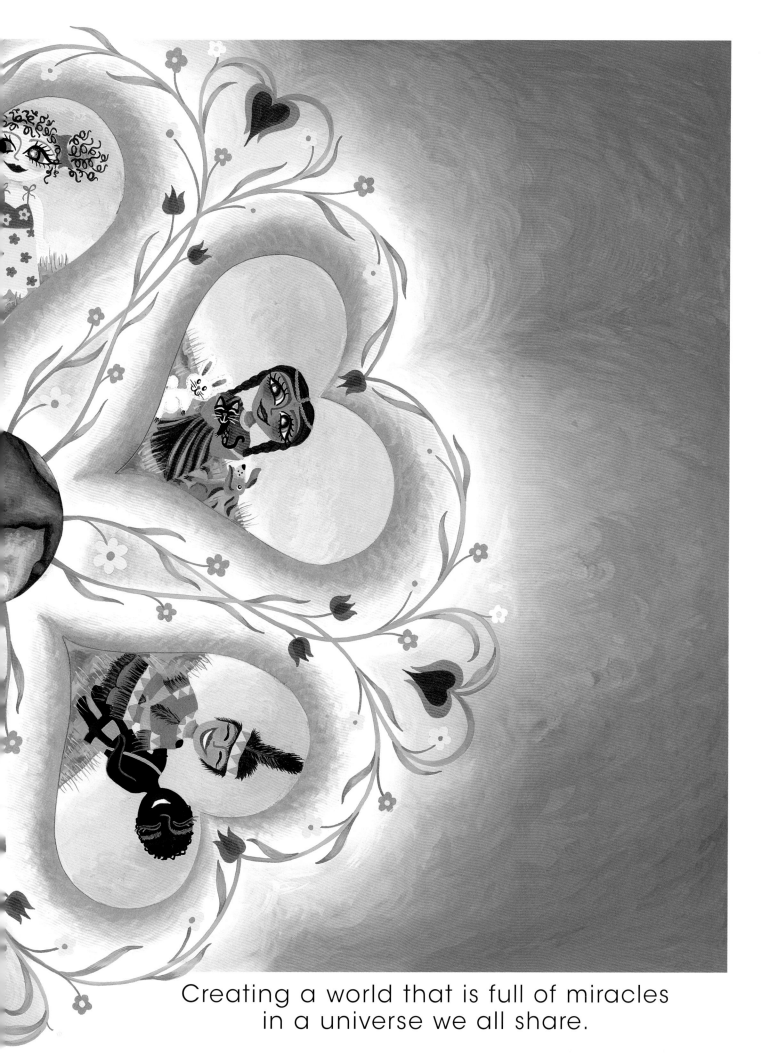

Creating a world that is full of miracles
in a universe we all share.

rainbow

earth

dog

So one thing to remember is...
We are all one but different.
Different but the same.

cloud

moon

pig   elephant

Created by the one light,
we are each given a name.

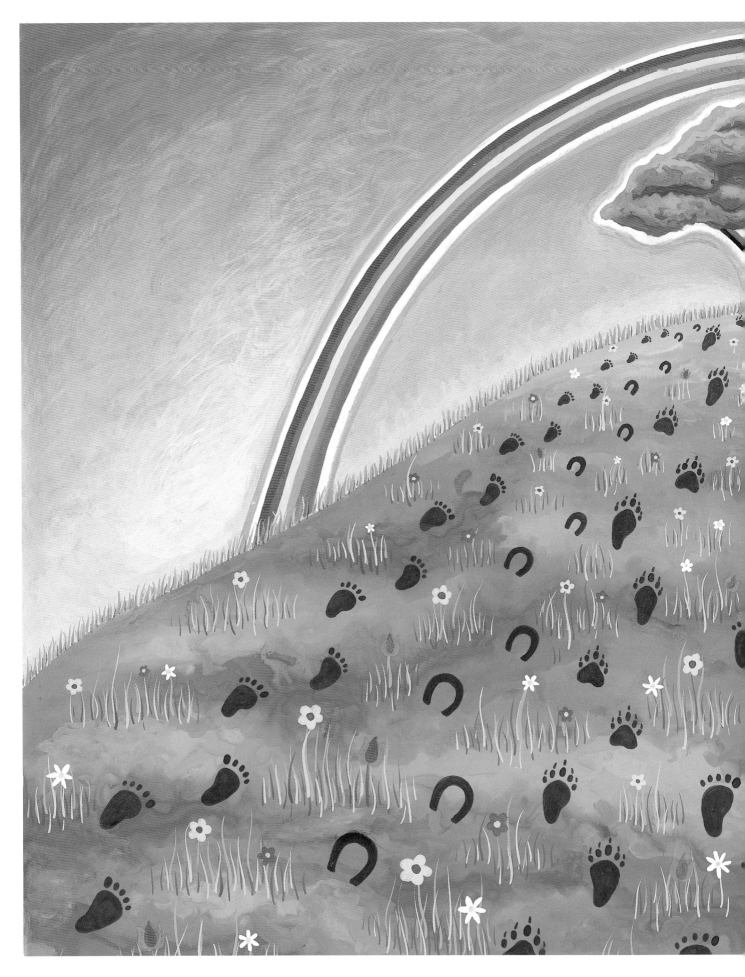

Walk lightly on this sacred land,

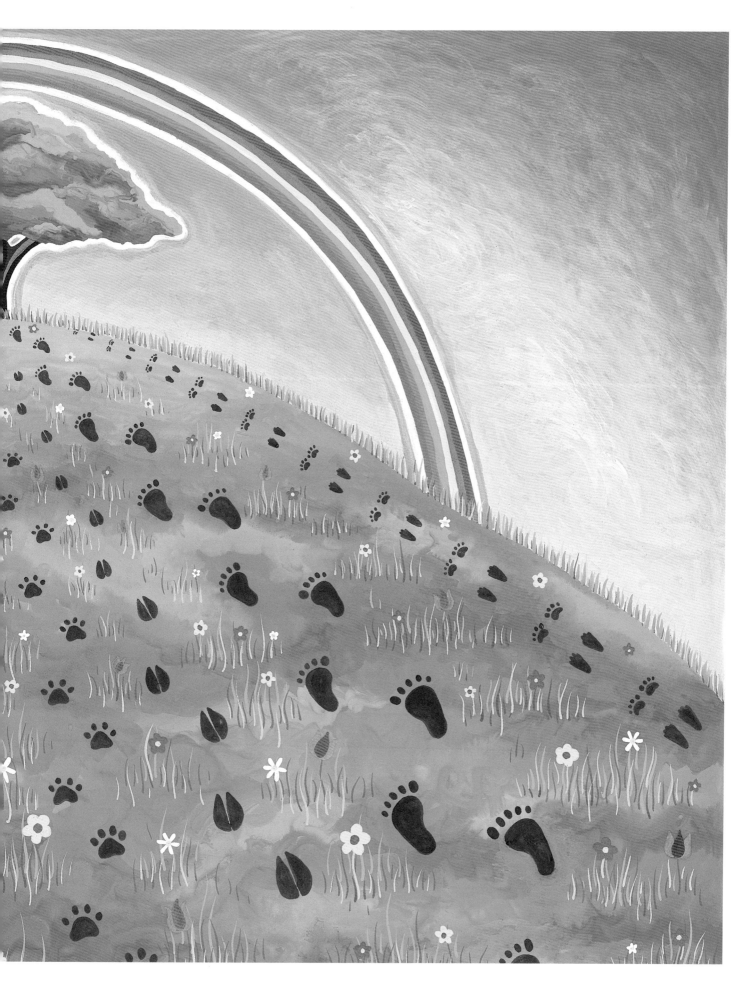

bless everything you see,

the light of love glows everywhere;

in every rock, every being, every tree.

The World of
We Are One

The World of We Are One is devoted to sharing messages
of unity and love that inspire us to honor and appreciate each other.

Our initial offerings come in the form of children's picture books, We Are One and *We Are Love*.

Through vibrant imagery and melodic verse, *We Are Love* explores the source
of love and shares how it can be experienced in our daily lives.

*'Love is the power of the universe. It shines through every star.
Love lights up everything you see. Love is who you are.'*

This message empowers and gently reminds us that the essence of life is founded
and created by *Love...*

To delve deeper into the virtues that support unity, compassion
and love, two sets of interactive cards have been created
We Are One Exploration Cards
We Are Love ♥ Journey of the Heart Cards

The World of We Are One intends to include various other mediums, such as music, visual arts,
interactive educational programs, DVD and multi media using a variety of like minded artisans.
For these products and more, please visit:
www.worldofweareone.com

ILLUMINATION
Arts

Published by Illumination Arts LLC,
140 Adams St, Quincy, MA 02169
info@illuminationarts.us   www.illuminationarts.us
Library of Congress Cataloging - in - publication Data
Library of Congress Control Number: 2010911712
We Are One / written and illustrated by Jennifer Black
Summary: We Are One is a children's picture book that reminds us
that whilst we may look, feel and see things differently, we are all the same.
ISBN 9-7809829225-0-7 (hardcover)
Published in the United States of America
Printed in China by Shanghai Kangshi Printing Co.,Ltd   2nd Printing 2010
Image Reproduction/Colour Management Clayton Lloyd - Flawless Imaging
Layout/Pre-press Vanessa Szychter - OpenArt Design